Responsibility

Natalie Sky Fix

N.S.F

Responsibility

This book is dedicated to my teacher Mrs. Walters.

Chapter One, The Morning.

1

"Bedtime!" Grandma calls.

"Grandma, it is still only nine at night; we are teenagers.
We don't have bedtimes anymore," One of the girls complain.

"Well, don't you want a bedtime story, Rose?" The grandma asks.

"We're too old for stories," Rose responds.

"Just sit." All three of them sit on the bed, "it is going to be a long story,"

"I bet it's about princesses," Josie whispers to her sister in a mocking voice.

"No talking." she warns. "a long time ago...

It's happening again. I wake up. It is two in the morning. I want to scream, but I can't. I feel eyes on me then I swear I hear breathing. I think I hear someone under my bed and I see a shadow of a man in the corner of my room. I take a deep breath, grab a blanket, and walk into the living room. I plop down on the couch and try to fall asleep. I see the living room light that has been forgotten about and left turned on. I finally fall into a dreamless sleep. I wake up to my brother getting ready for school around 7:00. I'm exhausted. I go back to my room and fall back asleep. It is 8:00 AM, and my alarm goes off. My body does not want me to move, but I stand up, ignore my headache and try to forget my uncomfortable night. I shower and get dressed in my dark gray jeans and my favorite blue sweater.

I make my way downstairs to the kitchen. My dad, a tall guy with balding gray hair, is sitting at the dining table drinking his morning coffee. I walk past him and wave. My brother, Grant, who has brown hair like me, is eating cereal next to him. I grab my backpack and head back upstairs to my bedroom.

While sitting at my desk, I rush to stuff all my papers and books into my school bag. Then I head out the door. I should stop by the old lady's house to check on her.

Nancy Hamilton is a woman that has been having trouble around the house because of her bad eyes. We usually sit and drink tea and talk about boring subjects such as the weather and how school is going. She used to be a storyteller when she was younger. Welp, this is my regular boing morning. My name is Ophelia, Lia for short; I know my name is different. My parents love William Shakespeare, so, of course, they had to name me after a dead character from one of his plays. I have crazy thick hair, dark brown eyes, and I am of average height.

"Hey, Mrs. Hamilton?" I call and knock on the front door.

The door opens, and she peeks her head out the door.

"Oh, hello dear, would you like some breakfast?" asks old Nancy with a kind voice.

"No thanks, I just ate," I politely reject. The truth is I didn't eat; I usually skip breakfast. Most people say that it's the most important meal of the day, but I disagree. Breakfast wastes time in the morning.

"Well, you should be off to school, dear," she tells me after we sit and drink tea.

"Dang it." I groan. School starts in ten minutes, I didn't realize how late it is, and I don't have my bike today. I left it at home. I begin to run to school, running against the fence separating the town from the forest. The school is right against the north side of the fence. Everyone that sees me tries to say hello to me. I wish there are other ways of transportation besides walking and riding bikes. I smile politely at the people and go on my way. The school is in my view now, and I slow my pace.

"Hey Lia, wait up!" here comes my idiot older brother.

Responsibility

"Why are you about to be late?" I question him.

"I'm not going to be late; I'm going to be right on my usual time." he smiles with a dumb sly expression on his face. "Well, you're still going to be late." The thing that interrupts our useless bickering is my best friend, Diane Henderson. She is a skinny girl with curly, ginger hair.

"My sister forgot her lunch," Diane says with an annoyed tone in her voice; she rolls her eyes and holds up a brown paper bag. "You guys know what today is, right?" I suddenly remember. I feel a shiver go down my spine. I try to hide my scared expression, so I give them a shaky smile. Diane looks just as I feel, terrified. Today is the day when 'old guy chooses your fate'; that is what my friends and I call it at any rate. I mean that the governor has one old guy pick paper from a large glass bowl.

He reads out the carrier listed on the paper for anyone that is sixteen through eighteen years old. Your age is depending on how much schooling you want. I am sixteen.

Grants 18, but he wanted to go at the same time as me. We rush to sign into the auditorium and take our seats. One by one, people's names are getting called and parents clapping right after.

Chapter Two, My Responsibility.

2

"Diane Henderson!" the old man calls. She is the seventh person called. He reaches into the bowl and reads from the small paper, "1st years school teacher." Her expression shows that she is pleased but at the same time frightened. She walks off the stage quickly, and more names are already getting called.

"Engineer!" then, "accountant!" Those are the most common jobs to get. "Sports coach!" and "Announcer!"

Then he finally calls out "Grant Waters!" my brother. I am burning with curiosity to see what job my brother gets. He is like almost everyone in this place, so he would fit right in with anything he gets. The announcer calls "Doctor." whoa, I would have never thought of him as a doctor with his foolish but caring personality. He will not be pleased with that.

Responsibility

I realize that my turn is next. "Ophelia Waters!" I stand up from my seat shaking, and I walk up to the stage. The announcer reaches his hand in the bowl that holds the hundreds of tiny pieces of paper that list all the careers. I feel a lump the size of an apple in my throat. The man opens the paper. He is frozen, the old man shutters; I think he is having a difficult time pronouncing this job. Is it that hard to say?

"Re-responsibilities," he says with a quiet, raspy voice. Why is everyone staring at me? What Responsibility? I look franticly around the crowd. I spot my parents. They look worried. Everyone bursts into whispers. "Ahem, Ahem!" The announcer says, trying to gather every one attention back, hoping they stay quiet. "Will the Waters family head to the church after the day's ceremony?" Grant gets out of his seat, but I cannot move. I stand there like a deer in headlights. Grant gets on the stage, pulls my arm, and we walk toward the doors.

We walk silently and sit side by side outside the church, waiting for my parents, who have to stay till the choosing of our fate's ceremony is over. They finally get here, and I rush to my mom's side.

"What's going on?" I ask. She says nothing with no expression on her face. I take a deep breath, trying to calm myself. As we walk into the church, I see the governor inside with a sly smile on his face.

"And here is the Star of the show!" he blurts out like he is in the middle of a conversation, yet no other individual is here, but my family and I.

"What's going on?" I ask

"You got the best job there is to get Miss.," he replies.

"What job? What do you mean?" I add.

"You, my dear, are going to answer and complete all my requests." he's known as an amazing, loving person in this place; he's quite the opposite.

"So, İ'm your maid?" I ask I'm discussed.

14

Responsibility

"No, you will have different jobs each day; a maid has the same tasks every day. Here's the best part," he continues with a wide smile. "If you don't listen, you get to watch your family disappear from right in front of you." I am in terror. He laughs darkly. If Grant isn't next to me holding up my arm, I will be on the ground. I feel lifeless. I can't say anything. I am in shock, "Well, good day to the family," he finishes cheerfully.

As he passes me, he whispers into my ear, "see you tomorrow Miss." he has an evil grin on his face. It's just now when I take notice of what he looks like. He has straight black hair that is greasy; you can tell he is very fond of himself by just how he's dressed, which is a white suit paired with a black tie and black shoes. He also has a fancy gold watch. I watch him while I am paralyzed with all the overwhelming emotions as he walks out the door. After a few minutes of silence, we all walk to our home. My parent still hasn't changed the expirations, and Grant is protectively watching me. He's always been like this. Once when I was eight years old, a kid stole one of my toys, and

Grant pushed him down. Many more times, this has happened but slightly different stories.

"Ophelia, Grant, time for dinner!" my mother calls for us. I don't move; I can't eat even though I am hungry. It is like there is a lump in my throat. It's like all the bottled-up emotions that I will never let escape.

I lay down on my bed and start to read the only thing that can fully calm me down, William Shakespeare's drama, *Hamlet*. It's about a young woman, Hamlet's possible wife, who, due to Hamlet's doing, ends up in a state of madness that ultimately leads to her drowning. It's not a very happy story, but it makes me feel somewhat safe. I fall asleep.

I suddenly wake up to a noise. There has to be something in my room corner even though I don't see anything; I hear my door rattle, Grant walks in. I'm crying, I can't see his expression on his face, there were too many tears in my eyes, so he just came in, shuts the door, and holds me till I'm done crying.

Responsibility

I fall asleep, but right before I did, I hear him whisper, "It's okay, Lia, I'm here for you."

I wake up; it's 7:30 in the morning, but there's no point in going back to sleep, so I will my horrible morning started. I shower and put on black leggings and a hoodie, brush through my hair and head downstairs. My brother is in the kitchen drinking coffee. I go to grab my backpack. Oh, I forgot. I don't have school anymore. The ceremony is always the last day of school. I shake my head at my forgetfulness. Instead, I bring my backpack upstairs, empty it, throw my wallet, a few books, and an extra sweater inside just in case it gets cold later.

I walk out the door, get on my bike and start peddling towards the beach. Two men in fancy suits stop me from going any further.

"Follow us to the boss's house." they have a stern expression on their faces. I'm confused. Oh, it must be the governor who wants me. I walk behind them, and It feels like I'm walking for hours. I am wheeling my bike next to me the whole time. I finally arrive. It is a huge beautiful house with a large willow tree in the front.

Chapter Three, The Boy.

3

As I walk inside the giant house, I see a boy around my age sitting on a couch reading. I cannot get a good look at him; the book is blocking his face. The governor walks into the room.

"You got her here successfully; you may leave now." the governor gestures to the huge men. "I hope you are hungry; I just had food made," he adds.

"I'm not hungry; I ate already," I snap at him.

"I'm not asking you to eat; I'm demanding you to eat!" he yells; he has a short temper. "Son, come eat!" The boy gets up quickly and sits down at the table. I do too, but I never left eye contact with the governor. I'm in a room with tall walls, a long table with a fancy chandelier above. An extremely thin woman walks into the room. She looks around fifty years old. She sets the food down at the boy's seat, then mine. She clenches her jaw as she goes around the table to the governor's seat.

"Why am I here?" I demand.

"Just eat," he returns.

"I'm not hungry!" The boy glances up as if he is worried for me; I should not say anymore. I start eating. I finely get a good look at the boy. He has messy black hair, gray eyes, and is slim. I look down at the plate in front of me full of all the breakfast foods that you can think of, pancakes, eggs, Tost, waffles, fruit, and more. It seems somewhat appetizing except for the thought of how the governor probably poisoned it; no, he most likely wouldn't. Stop, I think to myself. I can't look at anything but the governor. I have to focus. I don't want him to see me as weak; what will happen if I am weak?

"I'm done," I announce after I've picked at most of the food.

"Fine, Lorenzo, bring her to the sitting room," the governor commands. The boy simply nods, obediently gets up, and I follow him.

"You have to be careful. Don't test him. He will not hesitate to kill you and your family." he says in a quiet, rushed voice. I sit quietly. He has not said a word till now; I did not expect that.

"What does he want with me?" I ask.

"I don't know yet. Can you meet me tonight at the edge of the south fence?" he replies.

"Maybe, let me simply decide if I can even trust you first. What am I supposed to call your father?"

"Benjamin."

I nod and stay quiet. Lorenzo looks just as scared as I feel. Benjamin is walking into the room now. The boy shifts in his chair uncomfortably. It's his father, so why is he uncomfortable.

"So, Ophelia," he talks as if he's un-entertained. "That's a nice name, isn't it from the one poem with the William Shakespeare guy?" he seems relaxed as if he is talking to his friends or family. "Oh yes, she died from drowning. Well, that would be interesting to see, huh," he says in a bored tone.

I shiver; I am intimidated by his calmness. I trust the boy; he seems more scared of Benjamin than me, so I give Lorenzo a nervous nod when Benjamin looks away.

"Why did you want me here today," I ask.

"Well, your first responsibility is to get me something gold," he answers.

"Fine, when do you want it?" I say angrier than intended.

"Tomorrow night," he says with a smile. "Lorenzo, show Ophelia out." without question, I let him lead me out.

"When do you want to meet?" I murmur to him.

"Midnight." we nod. I walk down the long path that leads to the beach, and from the beach, I walk to my home.

Once I get inside, I say hi to Grant and go straight to my bedroom. I re-empty my bag and pack sneakers, a jacket, a flashlight, my book, a pocket knife, and a lighter.

"Ophelia, Grant! Dinner!" My mom made pasta for the meal, and I eat in silence and listen to their boring conversations.

"How was your day, Grant?" my mother asks.

"It was alright, you?"

"My day was great; I helped Mrs. Hamilton with some gardening before work, and then work went by quickly." my mom is a nurse at the hospital. "How about you, Kevin?" my mom asks my dad.

"it's been fine." I am not so hungry, so I just pick at my food with my fork.

"Goodnight, mom, good night, dad. I'm tired from the beach, so I am going to bed early." I say before they get to me.

"Goodnight, Hun." my mother replies. Grant's giving me an unconvinced look (I'm a terrible liar). I mouth to him to meet in my room. I rush upstairs and put on jeans and a flannel shirt.

"What is this about?" Grant asks, confused later this evening.

"I have to meet up with someone. I am so sorry for getting you into this, but can you make sure mom doesn't come in to check up on me?" I might have to beg. "Please?"

"Fine, you better tell me what this is about tomorrow," he says.

"Thank you. You are the best." I thank him. It will take around two hours to walk there; I walk out of my house at 10:00 pm.

"This is totally normal, just walking around in the pitch dark trying to meet a boy that I barely know," I tell myself sarcastically. An eerie feeling is creeping over me. I start running.

"Shush, you're being so loud!" someone whispers and scares me; I scream. Why am I so ridiculous? Who gets scared from a whisper? "It is just me, relax. Let's walk." Lorenzo adds.

"What do you want to talk about?" I ask.

"With Benjamin, you have to be careful about everything you do around him. Don't smile, but also don't frown. Speak only when spoken to, or you will get hurt and maybe worse, I swear to you." he blurts out all at once.

"How am I supposed to believe you?" I question him while trying to gather all that information. He gives me a frustrated look.

"I'm not exactly sure how to gain your trust, but please, believe me, I can't let any more people die." he winces as he says 'die.' Who died? Will I die? What about my family?

"So, what should I call you?" I ask.

"You can call me O, how about you?"

"Call me Lia, tell me about yourself." I say, "um, like, who is your mother?"

"Um, well, my mother died when I was young; what about your family?" he replies.

"Oh, I'm sorry for your loss. I live with my mom and dad. Do you have siblings?" I respond. I feel embarrassed for bringing his mother up all just to make conversation. Did I upset him?

"Nope, I'm an only child; I heard that you have a brother. What career did he get?

"Grant got doctor, what about you?" I claim.

"I don't get a career; I just get to be the boring governor one day. I guess it's passed down, and whatever, all I want is to be a writer or something exciting. It's lame, I know."

"Not really; I would definitely trade my career for something else. So, do you have any friends or family?" He gives me an 'I am sorry for saying that' look.

"None and the only family I have is my father. But I don't exactly count him as my family." I want to ask why but I shouldn't. "Did you find something gold yet?"

"Shoot! I completely forgot I have no gold at my house; maybe there's something at the school I can steal." I answer.

"Don't! Sorry, but don't steal anything, he will find a way to torcher you and your family, and that's way too easy for him." he hands a gold chain to me with a less panicky face,

"It's real gold, but it's not stolen or anything." We walk for another hour and talk. I start to shake. It's cold out, and I unintentionally left my jacket at home. "Here, you can take my hoodie," he says. "No, I'm fine," I say as convincingly as I can; he rolls his eyes, takes off his hoodie, and hands it to me.

"No, you will get cold," O replies, and he laughs.

"I have an extra," he says with a smile. I look down in embarrassment. We put the hoodies on quietly. Why wouldn't he give me the one he wasn't wearing? "Follow me; there's this cool spot I like to go when the stars are out." He speaks. I follow him reluctantly. We walk to a place with a little more than a dozen trees that have fallen, and there is a perfect empty spot between the trees. I'm in awe of the view of the Dark blue sky with millions of twinkling stars. I give him an approving smile. We lay on the hard ground in silence and watch the magnificent stars.

"Hey, look, a shooting star!" I say and look at O brightly; he grins.

"What did you wish for?" he asks right away. I never really thought about a wish.

"Nothing, I'm saving the wish till I'm ready to need it; what about you?" I answer.

"I am thinking the same thing," he replies. I look over to the watch on my wrist. Three hours had gone by.

"Dang it!" I'm always forgetting the time.

"What is it?" he asks with a cocked head.

"It's five in the morning. I have to get home in less than an hour somehow!" I complain.

"I have a shortcut; come with me." He leads me towards a path that should take me straight to the school then I can follow the fence to my house.

"Wait, what about you?" I am worried for him. My insides turn. Will his father, hurt him?

"Don't worry, he knows I'm not home; he thinks I'm clearing out this wood every morning." I feel my face loosen up.

I laugh with him.

Chapter Four, Fear.

4

"Lia!" Grant is practically shouting the moment I walk through my bedroom door. "Where have you been, and where did you go? Were you alone?" He's overreacting. I'm getting annoyed, but I know he's just worried. It's not like he hasn't been out till five in the morning, he's been out later than me, but when I stay out, it's a big deal.

"It's okay; I'm fine." I insist.

"Please answer at least two of my questions; where did you go, and were you alone?" he begs.

"I was with the governor's son, and all we did was walk around looking at the stars." He looks away with frustration. "Why were you with him?" He questions me.

"He was telling me how I can make sure our family doesn't get killed by Benjamin," I respond with annoyance.

"Who the heck is Benjamin? Why does he want to kill us? What does he want with you?" he continues.

"I'll answer your questions tomorrow. I am tired, and I'm sure you are too, so let's just go to bed; good night," I say and open the door for him; he looks slightly pale.

"Um, I guess. Good night then," he says with his eyebrows pulled together, and he walks out of the room, saying no more. I guess I should get ready for bed then. I unpack my bag, then I start to change my clothes. I put pajama pants on, and I toss the pants I was Wearing into the corner of my room. I'm still wearing O's hoodie, so I take the hoodie off, and I also throw it into the corner. I put on an x-large shirt that is super big. It is so big it pretty much fits like a dress on me. I climb into bed, and I fall asleep right away. Ugh. My brain won't shut up.

"Stop thinking," I tell myself. Finely I fall asleep.

Not tonight! I start to cry. I want to scream. Tonight's different than last night. I had a dream that I was dying from the old pandemic. All they were allowed to teach us in school is that it killed almost everyone in this place and no one else was the same after, it was nearly one hundred years ago, so there is no one to remember it. I close my eyes and try to fall asleep. I wake up, and my brother is already at school. The ceremony might have been my last day of school, but Grant now has to go to his final schooling classes. My parents are also at work, so I am going to be alone all day.

I head downstairs to grab a book from the bookshelf, and I get a glass of water. I run back up the stairs, not caring how loud I am, and I read for a few hours. I finish my water, take a shower, and get changed. It is around 5:00 pm now. I hear a knock on the front door, and I open the door slightly. O is standing on the front porch wearing a white shirt with a jean jacket over it, paired with dark blue jeans. He looks uneasy standing there. Why is he even here?

"What are you doing here?" I ask.

"May I come inside?" he questions me. I opened the door wider to invite him in. He walks in and shuts the door behind himself. O looks immediately eased to be inside. "Thank you."

"No problem, what are you doing here?" Why does he look so relieved to be inside?

"Benjamin wants me to tell you to go to his house around 6:00, and he wants me to walk you to make sure you don't hide or whatever," he says. He looks like he is in pain. I wonder if he might be hurt.

"Uh, Okay, Um, I need to get my book bag from my room. Are you waiting down here or coming with me?" I ask him stumbling over my words.

"Uh, I'll follow you, I guess." We headed up the stairs and into my room; I never really minded my room or even paid attention to it. But I suddenly feel slightly uneasy. It is not like my bedroom is messy or anything, but something about the thought of someone I barely know is about to walk into my room. I have boring tan walls with a twin-size bed in the far-left corner with one dresser in the right and a desk next to the door. I have a few posters with quotes on them and have a few paintings on the walls. We walk through the door. He does not look disgusted or appalled, but he looks... well, I think amazed.

"Wow, I only have a bed; my father doesn't let me have anything cool like that." He complements.

"Oh." I'm surprised; his father is so rich, unlike almost everyone in this place. "Sorry," I say awkwardly.

"Don't be sorry, I don't even spend a lot of time in there anyway." he sits on my desk chair that is in front of the desk. I grab my bag, and I put my pocket knife, wallet, a book, and an extra jacket inside.

"Oh, I almost forgot," I say, walking over to the corner of my room. I pick up the hoodie and hand it to him.

"Thanks, but you can have it," he responds.

"Why?" I am confused. Why does he want me to keep a hoodie that looks like it belongs to the richest person in this place? Well, it technically does belong to the richest person in this place.

"So, I leave my house with one hoodie and bring home two; how do you think Benjamin would react?" well, I did not think of that. I shrug and put the hoodie in my dresser. O and I walk to the house in quietness. We arrive, and we sit on opposite ends of the couch. Benjamin walks into the room and sits on a large armchair.

"You're finally here; give it to me," he demands me.

"Give you what?" I ask, dumbfounded, and I try not to show any emotions.

"The gold!" he yells angrily as if I insulted one of his favorite things. He reminds me of children's books with monsters called leprechauns. In the books, the leprechauns used to steal gold from something called a rainbow. A rainbow is a pattern of colors arranged as an arch shape in the sky. One time Diane claimed she saw a rainbow, but they don't exist.

"Here," I say in a calm voice, and I hand him the gold chain that has been kept in my pocket the whole time since O gave it to me.

"Where did you get it?" he asks aggressively.

I make up an answer as fast as I can. "Um, my grandmother gave it to me when I was young,"

"Okay, you can go home," he says in a flat tone.

"That's seriously all you wanted! We walked for an hour, and this is all!" I don't even know why I am so mad. I look to my right. I see O as he squeezes his eyes shut like he is in discomfort from hearing me raise my voice. Benjamin does not seem to notice. Benjamin walks over to me and slaps me. Not just a light slap, he used all of his strength.

"This is your first warning; I think you know what will happen if you get to three," he says with one eyebrow raised. "Lorenzo, go and show her around the house. You are horribly rude for not showing her yesterday. O winces.

"Yes, father." He gets up and walks towards the stairs; I do the same. We walk around the large house in silence until er go into a room that I'm guessing is his bedroom from what he described to me earlier—plan walls with a small bed in the corner.

"I can't believe you did that! Why?" he speaks in a hushed concerned tone.

"I'm so sorry; I don't know why I did that; I'm so sorry." I can't help but feel sympathetic toward him since he looked hurt from seeing me get a warning. We sit on the bed without talking.

Responsibility

"Can you meet me at the same spot tonight?" I want to say yes but would Grant even let me? I know I am my own person, but Grant is so protective and would be terrified that something happened to me. If I don't tell him, he would be up all night freaking out.

"I'm not sure, my brother is still upset that I left last night, and he's going to keep asking me questions about where I went and what's going on until he gets full answers."

"Bring him. We can tell him about what's going on tonight," he responds.

"I'll try." It is completely silent in the room for five minutes. I hear a knock on the door of his room. I jump; I hate random loud noises when it's silent in a room.

A man starts to speak, "Your father wants you to escort Miss Waters home." then I hear the man walk away.

"Is something wrong?" he asks. I'm guessing because I got scared, but I will avoid talking about things that freak me out.

"What do you mean wrong? Like wrong that someone is threatening to kill my family and me?" I question him, trying to look as annoyed as I can.

"Never mind, let's go," he says, scratching his head with confusion. He walks me home in silence and leaves me at the door.

Chapter Five, Fear.

5

"Hey, Hun, where were you?" my mom asks as I walk into the kitchen to get a snack.

"Nowhere, I just took a walk," I lie, and I take an apple from the countertop. "Is Grant home?" I ask, trying to seem unconcerned.

In his bedroom, I think, why do you ask?" she replies. My mom also looks upset.

"I'm just trying to make conversation, mom." I roll my eyes sarcastically and grin. "Is something wrong?" I'm curious but also worried. I hope my emotions do not show on my face. "No, I'm just a little tired; I think I'm going to go to bed early tonight. Do you think you can make dinner on your own today?" She does look quite tired.

"Yes, I'll make sure Grant eats too. Good night." I just want to go see Grant. I feel bad for my mom.; she is only usually only this tired if she is worried about Grant or me. Finally, I run up the stairs to Grant's room next to mine, and I walk in.

"Do you still want answers?" I ask Grant in a rush.

"Yeah! Finally." he sighs in relief.

"But you have to come with me, like out of the house tonight." he looks annoyed but nods his head in agreement.

"It will have to be quick. I'm meeting up with my friends to study early in the morning; I don't want to be exhausted." I am irritated, but we will still have plenty of time to explain most things.

"Fine, we leave at ten, and we have to walk fast." I leave the room and walk into mine. I repack what I had in my backpack from yesterday. I begin to walk back to the kitchen. I go to the countertop and grab a few apples. What will

Benjimen do next, and why is mom not saying anything about the ceremony? I read for the next few hours until I run up the stairs to Grant's room and knock on his door, "Come on, it's time to go." I call for him.

We walk at a fast step in the quiet darkness. We get to the corner of the fence and wait.

"Hey, did your brother come?" I hear O ask. he is not in my vision; it is too dark, and he is still a few feet away.

"Yes, I did," Grant responds before I can begin to answer. I roll my eyes even though no one can see my face correctly in the dark. O comes into our view.

"What do you want to know?" O questions respectfully.

"Everything," Grant answers.

"Okay, every year there is a choosing ceremony…" Grant cuts him off.

"Do you think I'm simple-minded? Skip to the part that

I don't know," he exclaims with raised eyebrows. O rolls his eyes.

"*I am* trying to tell you the things you don't know, so please don't interrupt." O takes a deep breath and continues calmly, "So, every year there is a choosing ceremony for not just jobs, but Its purpose is to choose someone to complete certain tasks for the governor." grant is looking annoyed.

"For the past 20 years or so, no one has got the job, well that is until Lia. That's why most people are surprised, and some don't even know what Responsibilities are. Benjamin is going to abuse that power. Well, he already is, I guess. If she doesn't do the tasks up to his standards, well, you already know what would happen. So, it's Lia's responsibility to keep everyone she loves alive. People think the job is like being Benjamin's secretary or maid, so no one knows how bad thing could turn." he concludes.

"Thank you," I say, trying to show him how much I care. I didn't want to be the one who had to explain to Grant for the third time.

"That's all? How come you were out for so long yesterday?" he directs towards me. He's red, and it seems he's trying not to seem concerned.

"We just walked around for a bit," I answer. It is true, and why does he have to be so protective?

"Okay, I should go home. I still have to meet up with my friends early in the morning. can you walk home yourself?" Grant asks me. A wrinkle appears on his forehead from worry.

"Yes, I'll be fine. See you at home." he leaves, and it is now just me and O. We walk to the tree pile again. We lie on the ground staring at the stars like last night.

"So, what are you going to once you get home?" O asks me.

"Nothing really. I'll probably go to sleep and then read; what will you do?" Now I'm curious.

"About the same thing. What are you going to read?" he asks, but I don't remember the title.

"I forgot the title, but it is about a farm and a girl; there was no fence like this place. She is free, and she can go anywhere she wants until something stopped her; I did not get the end of the book yet. What about you?"

"I've been reading William Shakespeare's Hamlet." I can't help myself. I start to giggle, but I stop myself. I feel the blood rush to my cheeks. He looks over at me and laughs. I draw an apple out of my bag.

"Do you want one?" I offer.

"Sure." we eat the apples in silence until he speaks again. "Do you ever wonder what is beyond the fence?" he bites his nails concentrating.

"Never really thought about it. Isn't it just trees and plants out there?" Now I am thinking about the fence. The fence is a large square around the whole place where everyone lives, and no one has ever been beyond the fence. No one has even attempted to climb the 30-foot-tall wire fence.

"Probably, but how are there no other people out there? It's just this small place. Also, why can't we go beyond the fence? The fence could not have magically appeared there, so who built it?"

"I'm not sure," I respond, shaking my head. The last thing I remember is that I am seeing stars before I fell asleep.

Responsibility

I dream about the forest, then I saw another fence

with a boy standing on the edge.

I tried to scream out for him to be careful, but I

cannot speak, he falls, and I can't say anything.

I wake up screaming. I am still outside. "What!" O yells while waking up startled. He sits up right away with his eyes still half-closed. He must have fallen asleep too.

"Nothing, I'm fine." his eyes are fully open, now looking frightened.

"Then why are you crying, and why did you scream?" I didn't realize till now that I am crying. I don't know how to answer his question; I can't just say 'I suffer from bad dreams and this is totally normal' because that's a ridiculous answer, but it's more than bad dreams, it feels like I'm going to get hurt or someone else will, but it starts and stops randomly, some times worse than others. I don't even know why I get these feelings.

"Nothing, I just had a bad dream." he doesn't look convinced.

"What's wrong? Please tell me," he begs with his eyebrows pulled together. "Please?"

.

"I don't know how to explain," we are now both sitting up and staring into the night.

"Let's go for a walk." he returns; I nod and get up. "What is this bad dream about?" he gives me a remorseful look.

"I don't know how to explain," I say with a serious expression. "I just get this..."

"Get this what? If you tell me, I can help or at least try to."

"Well, um, I get this weird feeling like I'm scared well more than just scared, like something bad is going to happen." I don't want to continue.

He raises his eyebrows as if to signal me to keep going. "It's a sickening feeling. Sometimes I wake up from it if I am sleeping, but also it makes me, well I don't really know." I look at him just to make sure that he isn't creeped out. His face is calm and reassuring; he notices that I am staring at him and gives me a tight-lipped smile.

"Where do you want to go now?" he sees right through me. He can tell there is more to say, but I don't want to continue.

"I don't know." so we walk around the tree pile a few times.

"Shoot, it's five; you should start to head home." he walks me home, and I go straight to bed. I am exhausted from being out at night.

Chapter Six, Fight—Grant's view.

6

I need to know what is going on with Lia. Was the governor serious that day? Who is that boy? Does Lia like him? What are the Responsibilities she has to complete? I need to walk to school. I can't be late for any of my classes anymore. This place takes final schooling very seriously. I also have to stop by old Nancy's home and check on her. I take a deep breath, and I collect all my school things. Once I have done that, I put my shoes on and rush out of the door. I walk over to Nancy's house and knock on the door.

"Mrs. Hamilton, are you home?" no answer. What's going on? Does she need help? Should I walk into her house? She's almost always home. I need to chill.

"I'm still alive, dear!" she yells from in the house. I swear I jumped ten feet in the air. "Grant, you know you don't need to come to check on me every day," she adds.

"Um, well, um, well, goodbye, I guess. Have a good day." shoot! How many times did I stutter? Is she judging me? Did she see how skinny I am? I eat a crazy amount, but it seems that I gain no weight.

Five years prior.

As I walk to school, I am holding my breath. Will Brian get there first? I speed up my pace. I'm in view of the school. I'm safe; he isn't here yet. I sigh in relief. I go around the school's side door, the quicker entrance to my classroom. I get pulled by my backpack, and my heart drops. Brian pulls me along to the back, where no one can see me.

"What's up, Grant? How you been?" he greets me with his evil smile. I open my mouth to say something, but he cuts me off. "Did you finish my homework as I asked?" he asks in a rush.

"I forgot I'm sor-" he punches me in the face and walks away, stomping in anger. He's two years older than me, so a lot bigger and stronger. The moment I think he's gone, he comes running back.

"How does it feel to be the freak?" he laughs. "You should go eat something before you die of starvation. You look like you haven't eaten in your who life. Bye, gaunt Grant." he takes my backpack and goes running.

I rush to the school. I'm running so close against the fence I hit my arm a few times. Why did that old man have to pick 'doctor' out of that damn bowl? I don't even know how to clean up a scratch after I fall. Knowing how I am already, I will have to repeat final schooling about a million times.

What's the point of me doing this? I wish there is a way for us to choose our careers. Most people in this place are poor, so what's the point of them picking our jobs. If we can pick our jobs, most people can make good decisions. If someone wants to be a nurse or a storyteller, they should get the proper schooling, but instead, the announcer can easily pick a garbage man. If we can pick our careers, Lia could be safe instead of herself and our family being in danger. She would not have met O. What type of name is just one letter? Is it short for something? Ugh. I arrive at the school.

I walk through the front door and into my class. While Mr. Brown marks us here, I open my notebook and start to doodle to pass the time. Once everyone is marked either absent or present, he begins his boring lecture. I stare off into space and occasionally nod to make it seem like I'm paying attention. I continue to do the same till class ends. Once I'm out of school, I walk home quickly.

Finally, I'm home from that dumb school. I set my backpack down on my bed that's in the corner of my room, and I lay on my bed. I just sit there staring at my ceiling. Not thinking, not talking, not doing anything but breathing. I finally get up after five minutes and walk downstairs. I get myself a glass of water and go back to my room. I pick up my backpack, put it on my desk, and start my homework. I don't understand one word of it. I shake my head and laugh in frustration.

I can't believe how stupid I am. Every 'doctor in training' or whatever knows all these answers. The moment the professor asks a question, every hand in the room goes up within 5 seconds, well, of course, besides mine. I wish I just got a sports coach or storyteller. All they need to know is how to be good with young children and how to read. I give up on my homework. I go back downstairs. I see Lia, who just woke up, is standing in the kitchen.

N.S.F

"It's 2:00 pm Lia; why are you just waking up?" I speak. "Um, well, I guess I was reading all night."

"I know you like to read, but not that much," I say with a cocked head. "How late were you out till?"

"I came home around two," she replies with an unconvincing expression.

"You're lying, I got home at two-thirty, and you weren't home." At this point, I'm shaking my head.

"Fine, I was out till five, I fell asleep," she tells the truth this time; she looks me in the eyes when she is being truthful. She shouldn't be around O; I don't trust him.

"Did you have any nightmares?" I say, trying not to show my worry. But she goes pale and ignores the question.

"How was your friend's house or whatever?" she asks and clenches her jaw.

"It was fine. What were you doing when I left?" I ask with a blank stare.

"We just took a walk, and I fell asleep."

"Did you have those nightmares?"

"No, don't worry about that stuff; it's nothing," she says while gritting her teeth.

"Why are you lying?" She is a poor liar.

"It's none of your business," she says, straining her voice to try not to yell. "Why are you so tired?" she continues with her eyebrows pulled together; she should not be thinking about me.

"I'm just tired," I replied blankly.

"Now, why are you lying?" she snaps right back at me. I roll my eyes.

"Are you sneaking out tonight again?" I ask and raise an eyebrow.

"Why do you need to know?"

"Am I not allowed to be curious?" I throw at her. Now she is raising her eyebrows. "Just tell me."

"I don't know if I am or not yet, I tell you later." she walks up the stairs then turns right towards her room. Why won't she be truthful to me? I need to get out of this house.

I walk out the front door and start to run to the beach. I need to think clearly. Why was she lying to me? What's going on? She had nightmares. Can O tell? Was he freaked out? How bad was the dream this time?

"Ugh!" I can't think straight.

Then I see him. He's just standing there doing nothing but staring out into the sky. I walk fast. I can't stop. I get to him.
He looks at me. I push him down to the sand.

Responsibility

"What the hell!" O yells. I kick him until my foot hurts. O pulls on my leg and brings me to the ground. He sits up, but he does not try to punch or kick me back; he just sits there calmly, covered in sand. with blood dripping from his nose, he asks, "What did I do exactly?" he asks angrily and crosses his arms. "Did I make your sister mad? If I did, how?" I cannot speak; I just lay there. O stands up, grabs my arm, and lifts me onto my feet. I take a deep breath.

"She said nothing. She looked, well, I guess embarrassed; what happened last night?" I blurted out all once.

"Nothing really, we walked around, talked and we fell asleep after. That's all, I guess." he looks at me but avoids eye contact.

"What happened when you guys woke?" I ask, trying to understand why she was lying.

"Nothing," he says and looks down at the ground.

"What happened? I'm not that dumb. Something had to happen for her to be lying to me." I throw at him.

"I said nothing happened!" he yells in frustration. It finally hits me; I'm dumb for not realizing right away. She doesn't want him to say anything.

"She had a nightmare again, didn't she." I flinch. O nods and continued to look at the ground.

"She didn't want me to tell anyone," he says defensively.

"Is she sneaking out again tonight again?" I ask.

"I'm not sure."

"What do you mean?" I'm starting to get frustrated again. He shrugs. "Is this another thing she is telling you to keep from me? Is she just going to show up waiting for you while you sit around? Are you going to the place you guys decide to meet up just in case she does decide to go? Are you just going to ditch her?" I'm raising my voice now.

"I'm going to the spot where we usually meet up and wait there until five. I'll go back to my place if she does not sow um.

Is that fine for you? Or do I have to ask for your permission?" he asks sarcastically. I roll my eyes, keep a blank expression, and turn to walk home.

Chapter Seven, Frustration.

Lia's view.

7

I sit on my bed quietly, listening for the front door. Why was he so angry? He's not the one who has to protect everyone. I hear the door open. I feel my face go pale, and I walk out of my bedroom. I peek down the stairs and see Grant. His face is red, and he's practically shaking in anger. Why is he so mad? Is he mad at me? I walk back to my room in silence. My heart is pounding. Did I make him mad? This has to be my fault. He hates me now. I shouldn't have lied.

My breathing is heavy. I fall to the floor. What if I end up killing my family by not listening to Benjamin? Or even just miss hearing him. Am I going to tear my family apart before that? I CAN'T BREATHE! My chest hurts. Tears are rolling down my face. Am I dying? If I die, what happens to my family! My head is screaming. Grant comes bursting into my room.

Thank gosh, my parents are at work; I don't want them to see me like this.

"Why did you L..." he starts and stares at me dumbfounded. Is he frozen? "What happened? Are you hurt?" He is just as pale now. I think he's shaking, or am I shaking? I can't speak. "Please talk. Please!" He looks terrified. "What do I do?" he's repeating himself. Grant is pacing around my room as if trying to find an answer to what he can do to help. "Should I take you to the hospital?" his gaze is directed down towards me. I shake my head.

Trying to find my voice, I say, "No. no. I'm fine." I'm at least not gasping for air anymore. My eyes are squeezed shut. "Go," I'm trying to slow my heart race now. "I'm fine." I open my eyes, and he is wincing like in pain. "Are you alright?" I question him back.

"I'm fine, don't worry about me." he fires at me.

"Well, I am going to worry. Tell the truth."

"I'm fine. Are you sure you don't need to go to the hospital?" he looks very concerned.

"I'm just great," I say in a sarcastic tone. "Go, I have to do something." Grant looks hesitant at first.

"Well, ok, fine." he heads out of my room, and as if on purpose, he leaves my door open. I close the door as soon as he walks out of the room. I grab my backpack and put the same things as usual inside. Book, pocket knife, hoodie, wallet, and my notebook and pen. I put on my shoes and headed to my mom's room.

"Hey." my mom says and looks up from her desk.

"Hey, you don't care if I sleep over at Diane's house, right?" I ask.

"Of course, Hun. Just remember to check in with me tomorrow," she tells me. She looks stressed. It must be from work.

I head out the front door, but Grant stops me in the middle of the path.

"Where are you going?" he questions me. Yet, I don't know that answer fully myself.

"Um, to Diane's house, I'm sleeping over there." I try to sound as convincing as I can.

"I'll walk you then," he adds. His face shows he's that not dumb enough to fall for my lies.

"Get off my back," I snap at him right away; I'm getting agitated. I walk away without looking back, against the fence, trying to find somewhere to go.

I've been walking for about half an hour when I stop in my tracks. The same two men are there.

"What do you two idiots want," I say even though I know it's Benjamin who wants me.

"Come with us." the man on the left says.

"Why can't Benjamin bother me on a different day," I complain without moving my feet to follow them. Then I recite all the things O told me to do and not do, I remade my decision. "Fine, let's go already." I sigh.

Once we arrive at the house, the men lead me to the living room and left. I sit on a couch. Benjamin walks in and sits in the chair that is in front of me.

"So, would you like another Responsibility?" he asks me.

"I would say no, but I don't have a choice, do I now?" I shake my head and laugh darkly. I raise one eyebrow. "What do you want?" my tone and expression go serious again.

"Well, I guess to cut things short, I want a pocket knife and a picture frame," he says. I'm shaking my head.

"So, you want me to get you stuff that you can get anyone else here to bring you?" I knew the answer, but it sounds so ridiculous. I open my backpack and take the pocket knife out and toss it to the man standing behind Benjamin. "There, you happy? I'll come back tomorrow for the frame." I walk out of the house without turning my head to look back. Is serious? I am halfway down the path when O catches up with me.

"Hey! Slow down." he grabs my arm to stop me.

"Stop!" I am extremely frustrated and not even at one particular thing. I pull away from him and continue walking.

"Where are you going," he asks while trying to keep up with me. I ignore him. "Did I make you upset?" his voice sounds calm and uneasy at the same time. "Please answer me." I roll my eyes. "I'm just going to keep following you, you know." I finally look up at him. He had a black eye, and his nose was a mix of red and purple. I stop and stare.

"What happened?" I ask anxiously.

"Your brother happened," he says without making eye contact.

"What!" I exclaim.

"It's nothing, never mind about me. Why are you mad?" he asks.

"I'm not," I say truthfully. We are close to the tree pile now. His eyes go wide for a second, but he regains his calmness.

"Then let me rephrase, why are you upset," he replies loudly. I roll my eyes.

"I don't know," I add truthfully. He looks exhausted. "When was the last time you got any sleep?"

"When did you last sleep?" he throws right back at me. I got plenty of sleep; it's when I felt like I was dying; all that sleep seemed to disappear from time.

"Why does Benjamin need all these random things? A pocket knife, a picture frame, and a gold chain." I say, thinking out loud.

"I'm not sure; I think he is just trying to taunt you," he claims.

Chapter Eight, A new mindset

O's view.

·

8

I can't believe Lia. She got no sleep at all. Her eye bags are a pale bluish color. I also can't believe she did not expect that from her irrational brother either.

"Hello? Are you listening to me?" Lia is talking; I have to Focus on her.

"I'm sorry, what did you say?" she looks at me, shakes her head, and grins.

"Well, I said, I'm going to be out here all night. I'm sure that you don't want to hang out here that whole time." I laugh darkly; I would have been here anyway.

"I'm sure I'll survive," I answer. She looks at me with a confused face but drops it right away. Most of the time, I'm here anyway; it won't make a difference. I smile to ease the tense mood in the air. We both sit on one of the dozens of old fallen trees that no one is going to bother moving. Except that Benjamin thinks I been clearing out this wood.

I hope every day my so-called father never comes to check up on how much I have done, well more like hasn't done. Knowing Benjamin, he would send some middle-aged bald guy in a suit to check for him. I should consider taking care of at least some of this wood. I've been having this weird thought in my head that has been bothering me for a while now.

"What do you think would happen if someone leaves here and goes beyond the fence," I ask.

"Like I said last time, I don't know." she is lying down on her back, looking at the clouds.

"I did not ask that question; last time I asked you what you thought was out there, this time I'm asking what you think would happen if someone goes out there." I point out. She laughs.

"My answer still stands." she looks peaceful. If Benjamin ever hurt her, I don't know what I would do without her; I just know I won't be here for much longer if she's ever gone. From the moment I saw her, I knew I cannot let him have complete control. I shake my head.

"What?" Lia asks.

"Nothing, I'm just thinking." she looks puzzled but then turns her gaze from my face back to the sky. We sit there for about an hour. She stares at the sky, and I stare at her. She finally sits up and reaches into her backpack. Lia pulls out a book and opens it to the first page.

"What's that?" I ask. She smirks.

"A book," she answers ironically. I laugh—a genuine laugh.

"You know what I mean." we stare into each other's eyes for a whole minute before she answers.

"It's called, To be a Monster." She looks content and excited to read.

"Will you read me some?" I ask, curious to see what's hidden beyond the covers of the book. She smiles shyly.

"Fine," she says, chuckling. She finally opens the book and starts. *"once Apon a time a witch..."* she has been reading for around an hour when I fully zoned out. How can one single girl change my thoughts completely when I'm with her?

"Are you listening?" she asks.

"Yeah."

"Well, you look out of it to me. What was the last sentence I said then? I smile. Fortunately, I was listening at the last second.

"get over here; I need answers." I quote, and I'm quite amused by her amazing confused brown eyes.

"How-" she just laughs and moves on. We stop reading and sit there doing nothing.

"Why are you staying here tonight?" I ask curiously. She looks up at me.

"I just needed to clear my head in peace," she admits.

"I understand that feeling," I say under my breath.

"What was that?" she asks, not fully hearing me. I laugh even though I don't have a reason to.

"Nothing," I say. She looks confused and curious.

"Come on, what did you say?" she says and stands up in front of me and puts her hands on her hips.

"I said nothing." she pursed her lips. I stand up next to her.

Responsibility

"Until you actually tell me, I'm just going to assume whatever you said is worse than you did say," she says with a mocking smile. I roll my eyes. "What did you say!" she vocalizes. I roar with laughter. She rolls her eyes back and gives up. We both went to lay on the grass to watch the clouds.

I hear screaming. I bolt up from the ground. I shake Lia awake. "What's wrong? What happened?" I ask frantically. She cries and tries to speak, but it's inaudible. I just hold her. Her breathing finally slows. She's asleep. The moon shines on my watch. It's two in the morning. I can't fall back asleep; I can't wake her. She looks cold. I slowly take off my hoodie and lay it over her. I am cold, but I slow my breathing to try to prevent myself from shaking. I wonder what she was dreaming about.

Chapter nine, The Dream.

Lia's view.

9

I feel cold. I see a young boy. He looks a little older than five years old; he can't be older than seven. He has black curly hair and grey eyes. Is that O? He is running. Peaceful. Happy. Bright. I can hear his laughter. Suddenly it's dark. He calls out for anyone. "where are you? It's too dark; I can't see." I call back.

"Help!" he screams. The light is back but dim. I look around and I can't see him.

"Where are you!" I yell out. Everything is different when this new light came. It's this place. I see the fence. The boy is balancing on the top. Benjamin is standing next to him holding him by his shirt.

"Put him down!" I screamed. The boy squirmed.

"As you wish, ma'am," he says calmly. He drops the shirt of the boy. He balances there for a few seconds before losing his balance. He falls. I see him get up. He is on the other side of the fence, Luckily not badly harmed. Benjamin is gone now.

"Climb, can you climb the fence?" I yell at him.

"No, help me, please." he is crying.

"it will be okay," I reassure him trying to calm him down. He turns around.

"Bad men. Bad men!" he screams.

"Climb!" he starts his way to the fence, but his legs are too short. The men got to him first.

Responsibility

"No!" I scream.

"What's wrong? What happened?" O asks franticly. I try to speak, but I'm crying too much for any full words to come out of my mouth. He holds me tight, and I don't move. I just lay there. "It's okay, love, you can sleep. I'm here." I finally slip into a dreamless sleep. I start shivering, but I warm up soon after somehow. I wake up a few hours later. O's still awake. Where is his hoodie? He must be cold. I look down at myself. He put his hoodie over me.

"You must be freezing," I say while turning back and handing him back the hoodie.

"I am fine," he says with one hand on the hoodie. I ignore him and push the hoodie further into his hand. This time he does not deny. I stand up. How did he not run away from me last night? I shake my head.

"Would you like to go and get something to eat?" he asks me politely.

"I kind of can't go anywhere where people can see me. My family thinks I'm at my friend's house at this moment." he squints his eyes in confusion but does not comment.

"Come on, I know where to get food without people seeing us," he adds. We start walking to the opposite end of the fallen trees. I've never been over this way before; I don't think anyone ever goes this way either. "What's up with the lying? Is it about your brother?" he asks.

"Well…" I would try to deny it, but he is not wrong. I just nod my head. "Where are we going?" I ask him.

"To my friend, Suzen's, house," he answers automatically. I stop dead in my tracks.

"Excuse me? Didn't you hear me say no, people?" I question him.

"Relax, she used to be like one of the maids at Benjamin's place." Does he think that's better? Then I remember my dream. Benjamin. I shiver. Why does he only say it's Benjamin's house?

"No," I say assertively. I feel sick.

"It's okay; she despises him more than anyone else in this place." that does not help. "She was not so lucky when it came for her to pick her job like you. But it ended worse for her; she did not complete one of her responsibilities." I breathe in a sharp jagged breath. "I think you know what happened." what he says still doesn't help. I have a bad feeling about her.

"Fine, but I'm waiting outside," I say, frowning. He nods, understanding how I feel. We walk behind a few old empty buildings for a while. I see only one building with a light on and slowed my walking. "Is that the building?" I ask.

"Yep." he looks at me, waiting for approval to keep going. I nod. We get to the back of the building, and he knocks on the door.

"Lorenzo? Is that you?" I hear an old lady call out.

"Yes," I hear a few locks turn. "Are you still waiting out here?" he asks me quietly. I nod my head.

"Yes," I reply. The door opens.

"Who's the girl?" Suzen asks firmly.

"A friend of mine," he responds to her. "Would you mind sparing us a few apples?" he asks politely.

"Come on inside." the woman says. I look up at O. He gives me a quick smile.

"I'll be right back," he says quietly enough for me to hear, but not Suzen. He walks through the door with her. I feel my heart start to race. I sit on the ground with my head between my knees, taking deep breaths. Finally, after what seems to feel like forever, the door opens. I stand up right away. And walk to O's side. He looks at me, worried. Then, he turns to Suzen. "Thank you," he says to her and gives her a polite smile.

"It's no problem. Come visit again soon; it was nice

seeing you," she replies. She's tall, and she has a large scar across her neck. She might be around 50 years old.

"Same to you," he responds. We walk away. Once we are out of the building view, he asks, "Hey, are you okay?" He has a concerned look on his face.

"I'm fine," I say. He looks unconvinced but shakes it off. Once we get back to the tree pile, he took a couple of apples and a few muffins out of a bag. We eat quietly. I am sitting back on one of the trees when I suddenly remember. "Shoot!" I exclaimed. "I still need to get him a picture frame." I sigh. I don't want to leave. I don't want to face Benjamin.

"Well, let's go then," O responds. "He would expect me to get you from your house anyways." he sighs. "Do you have one yet?"

"Yeah, but it's at my house," I say, feeling guilty that he has to walk that far with me.

"Well, let's go then," he says with a smile. I smile slightly back. We arrive at my house. All I see is everyone standing in the living room through the window.

"Shoot," I say. I feel the color leave from my face.

"What is it?" he asks and looks concerned.

"Everyone should be at work or school." I take a deep breath in and out Shakily.

"It will be fine. Should I come in or wait outside?" he asks.

"I think it would be best for you to wait out here," I say with sympathy. He smiles politely. He leans against the wall of the house, and I walk inside.

Chapter Ten, Lies.

10

I walk through the door, and I look back at O. He nods to reassure me that he will be there. I take a deep breath and walk towards the living room.

"Ophelia!" my mother yells to me.

"Where have you been!" my father asks strictly.

"Diane's house, like I said," I respond as fast as I can.

"Why are you lying?" my mom questions me.

"What do you mean?" I ask innocently. Grant sits quietly in the chair next to me.

Responsibility

"I wanted to see you this morning because I had no work; you weren't there." my father says. I go as pale as snow.

"I'm very sorry. I will not lie again." I try to walk away, but my mom stops me.

"You are grounded." my mother says.

"I understand that, but I have to go somewhere right now. I will do any punishment you want me to do when I get back." I respond. I try to walk away again.

"No, you are staying here in this house!" my father raises his voice at me.

"I'm sorry, I have to go." I wince as my voice breaks. I have rarely heard my father yell. But I know what Benjamin would do if I don't show up. Grant understands my uneasy tone of voice. He stands up.

"Let her go," Grant tells them. They ignore him. I walk away anyway. I do not look back, scared to see their faces, scared if I broke down. I walk to my room, grab a random picture frame from my desk, take out the photo, and throw the frame in my bag carelessly. I walk down the stairs and out the door. I don't wait for O to say anything, and I can hear my parents arguing in the kitchen. I feel my face go red. Tears of anger roll down my face. Not at my family, but Benjamin. Why is he doing this to me? Did I do something to deserve this? My head feels like it's about to explode with anger.

"Slow down, Lia," he says. "Slow down." He says again. He can easily see that I am frustrated. He stands in front of me to stop me from walking. I step around him. Once again, he stands in front of me; this time, he puts his hands on my shoulders. "Your family will forgive you." I don't speak. I am afraid I will break down if I opened my mouth. My head feels warm. "You will be fine, as well your family," he reassures me. I attempt to calm down just enough for me to try to finally talk.

"This is going to happen again. I have to keep lying to them to protect them. They don't understand that. One wrong move, and he will kill them." my voice keeps breaking. I thought I was calm enough, but I'm not. I start to break down and sob.

He holds me in his arms.

"It's going to be okay." he tries to calm me. "I will protect you and your family. I won't let anything happen. But you need to try to calm yourself. We have to face Benjamin. Everything will be fine." I nod. I take a deep breath and pull away from him. He doesn't reassure me, but I give in.

I start to walk again. I wipe my eyes to try to hide any trace of tears. Will Benjamin notice? We walk past the beach. I look over to look at the view, but O does not even glance over. Is O nervous about facing Benjamin? We got close to the house, and O went unusually pale.

"Are you okay?" I ask him. He does not talk. He just nods his head to indicate that he is. I do not believe him.

"Remember to stay calm and don't irritate him," he tells me. We walk up the steps. He moves a few feet further from me.

We sit down in the living room and wait. Is he scared of what Benjamin could do to us?

"Well, hello, Ophelia," Benjamin announces; O jumps. Only I seemed to notice. I look at O; he will not look me in the eyes. "Thank you, Lorenzo. You can go now."

"He can stay, I don't mind." I croak. I look up at Benjamin.

"Well, if you say so. He may stay." Benjamin says. O nods, "Did you get what I asked?"

"Yes." I open my bag and hand him the picture frame. "Is this good enough for you?" I ask him. It's a plain black rectangle frame.

"Yes, join us for dinner now." O looks up, admittedly.

"I'm very sorry, but I need to get back to my house," I respond.

"Fine. walk her home." Benjamin advises O. We walk quietly, and we are halfway to my house when I start shaking in anticipation of how my family is feeling. O stops.

"It will be okay; your family loves you; they will always forgive you." I nod. O makes me feel safe.

"Do you have to leave?" I don't want him to go. He frowns.

"I would much rather stay with you." he gives me a quick tight-lipped smile.

"um, would you like to stay over here for the night?" I ask him nervously.

"Only if you're fine with it," he adds. His eyes seemed to brighten when I ask.

"Okay, when I go inside, go around to the back of the house, and wait ten minutes. My brother is going to want to check on me, then I'll let you in." I say, thinking of a plane as fast as I can.

"Okay, are you telling your brother?" he asks and shifts uncomfortably.

"I'm not going to tell him. If he finds out, you will end up with worse than a black eye." I shake my head and laugh nervously.

"Okay." he agrees. Once we were close to the house, I give him a nod to head to the back. "I'll see you soon." I give him a tight-lipped smile. I walk inside, focusing on my breathing, trying to stop shaking.

"Hey." my mother interrupts me from walking too far into the house. "I'm not sure why you had to leave, and I don't care; you are grounded for the next month. You are not to go out unless you have a real reason." I nod and continue my way up the stairs towards my bedroom. I finally get in my room, and Grant barges in.

"Why did you lie?" he demands.

"I had to," I answer.

"I asked why." he urges.

"I said I had to; I'm tired, please get out," I say right away. He hovers over me for a moment before leaving. I lock the door behind him and open my window. "Hey," I whisper too. O. he looks up. "Grab that Ladder." There was a ladder left out from my dad fixing part of the roof. He moves it over and starts to climb up. I help him inside, and we both sit on my bed.

"How was your family?" he asks worriedly.

"My mom was okay; I did not see my dad. Grant was well, Grant."

"Well, let's hope I don't get a second black eye tonight." he has a broad smile now. I cannot help but grin back. "Will you read again?" he asks.

"Um, sure," I say, unsure at first. I pull out the book and start to read. After an hour or so, I begin to yawn.

"Do you want to stop? You seem tired," he says.

"No, I'm fine," and I continue to read. After a few minutes, my eyes start opening and closing slowly, struggling to stay open.

"Let me see the book," he says. As we both lay on the bed, O reads to me. I close my eyes and listen. I drift off to sleep soon after.

It's the same dream again. The boy that looks like O. The bad men. Benjamin. But this time, he escapes from the men. It's completely bright again. The boy runs to me. He's happy, and he is laughing.

"Thank you," he tells me. I smile worry-free. We run around in a beautiful meadow playing. He tells a million stories of adventures and journeys. I feel happy. I feel safe.

I wake.

"What are you doing on the floor?" I ask O, who seems to be awake.

"Someone decided to take the whole bed," he says in a joking tone. "It's your bed, not mine; it would have been rude of me to stay," he adds politely.

"You should have woken me; I would have slept on the floor" I feel guilty. I realize I did not wake all night. I didn't even have a bad dream. I don't remember when I had a good dream; it's either bad or no dream at all.

"It was no problem; I slept all night," I smile at him. I hear the door rattle, and my heart drops.

"Lia? Are you awake?" I look at O frantically.

"Um, uh, y-yeah," I call back.

"Why is the door locked?" Grant asks.

"Uh, I'm getting changed; what do you need?" I respond.

"Well, I'm off to school. Mom and dad are at work. Don't go anywhere, or you will be in more trouble than you already are." he informs me.

"Okay," I say. "Since when are you the responsible one?" I say too quietly for him to hear.

"What did you say?" Grant asks.

"Nothing, I said nothing," I respond, trying hard not to laugh. I heard O chuckle quietly. I kick him softly to warn him to shut up.

"Promise me, Lia," he asks earnestly.

"I promise. Just go. See you later." I say, trying to end this conversation.

"Um, okay, I guess goodbye then," he says back. I watch him leave the house from my window. And I burst out laughing.
I can't believe I did not get caught. O smiles.

"What's so funny?" he asks, amused by me.

"Nothing." He looks at me with a crooked smile.

"I see how it is, I would not tell you what I said the other day, and now you won't tell me what's so funny huh," he says sarcastically. I giggle, unlock my door and head out of the room.

"Do you want something to eat?" I ask him.

"Sure," he responds. He follows me to the kitchen. I take a few apples and a few pastries from the pantry.

"Is this fine?" I ask him, not knowing what he likes.

"That's perfect," he answers. We eat at the table quietly. There has been a question in my head for a while now.

"Why did Benjamin keep Suzen alive? He killed her friends and family, but not her?" I ask out of the blue.

"I think Benjamin understands that death is by far better than losing everyone around you," he answers. "What's the point of living if there is no one to give you a reason to," he answers like he knows what that fees like. I am curious why he responded in such detail, but I do not comment. I stare out of focus, thinking and letting my thoughts take over my mind.

Chapter Eleven, Blue Sapphire.

11

We sit in the Livingroom taking turns reading until the book ends.

"That book is going on my top ten favorite books list," he declares, and I smile. We talk about our favorite books for the next hour, and I tell him about my friends. "So, what should we do today?" he asks.

"I'm not sure; Grant gets home around three," I add. He nods. There is knocking at the door. I look at O. He gets up and goes into the hallway for me to see who's there without him being caught. I open the door, and the two men are there.

"What," I say automatically like I don't already know.

"Benjamin wants you." the man on the right says. I sigh. O shows up next to me. The men look bewildered.

"I was already getting her, you idiots. Leave," The men nod and turn around. He seems to be braver in front of them than his father. Is it because they can't hurt him? Has his father hurt him before? I close the door.

"Do you know what he wants this time?" I ask him.

"No clue." he sighs. I go upstairs and throw everything inside my bag, including a new book from the bookshelf. We are halfway to the house, and we spot Grant on the path in front of us.

"What are you doing out?!" Grant exclaims.

"Um, well, uh, I just have to go somewhere," I respond.

"What's he doing here?" Grant barks.

"He's walking me to the place I need to go to,"

"You could've told him I can walk you." he declares.

"Hey, would you have liked her to walk by herself?" O speaks up. Grant looks at me, aggravated.

"Where are you going," Grant asks.

"None of your business," I answer.

"Sorry, but we are not allowed to tell you," O says in a tone as if he was correcting me. Grant acts like he is not there.

"I'll see you later," I reassure and step around him.

"Lia..." Grant continues but drops the conversation. We keep walking in silence.

When we arrive, two more men stop me from walking in.
"He's busy right now." the man that is on the left side of the doors says. The other man hands me a paper.

"Now leave you." the other man adds. He must have got no schooling; he sounds like a toddler. All most everyone gets schooling. "In Benjamin wants you," he says, directing to O. We walk down the driveway together.

"See you soon," he tells me. I frown.

"Can you come back later?" He gives me a quick smile.

"I'll try," he adds. "Goodbye,"

"Bye," I reply quietly. I walk back to my house and go inside. Will O be okay.

"What the hell." Grant objects. I ignore him and go straight to my bedroom. I sit at my desk and open the piece of folded paper the men gave me.

"Dear Ophelia-

You are on your last strike. There is no reason you deserve all three. (I can imagine him smiling with his stupid grin.) *Here is a list of things you need to get me before*

Saturday the 23 (it's the 16th.) *Make sure you leave the whole day open so you can stay for dinner.*

List:

1 rose.

1 bottle of paint.

A children's book.

1 glass jar.

A child's toy.

1 bracelet.

A rope.

1 hairclip.

A watch."   *-Benjamin*

I sigh. Does he really need all this crap? What even were the first two strikes? My mom and dad come home from work, and we sit at the table and eat dinner silently; I feel horrible that I disappointed them. I went to my room to read a book. I hear a knock on my window. I shriek, being frightened. It is just O. I can see him laughing. I open the window and help him in.

"Was that amusing?" I ask in an annoyed tone. He laughs harder.

"Kind of," he responds. I roll my eyes but grin.

"What was that!" my brother yells from the other side of the door.

"Uh, nothing, I just fell," I answer. I hear him stomp his way back to his bedroom. I shake my head and chuckle.

"What did Benjamin write?" he asks, being cautious of how loud his voice sounds this time. I hand him the note, and he had the same reaction as me and sighs. "Well, at least it's things you can find easily," he says.

For the rest of the night, we read and talk about other books we have read. He likes to read realistic fiction. I notice he is wearing a necklace. It was a gold chain with a blue sapphire at the end.

"What's that?" I ask curiously. He looks at it and holds the sapphire in the palm of his hand.

"It was my mother's," he responds; he has glazed eyes. I wonder what's going on inside of his mind?

"What happened to her?" I ask, hoping I don't offend him.

"She passed from a disease when I was ten," he answers and looks ashamed and doesn't look me in the eyes. "her name was Elizabeth Lee." I nod and listen to his every word. "I look like her, and she also loved to read." he smiles.

I remembered my dream. A young boy that looks like him is running in a meadow. I smile from thinking of the happy boy running around smiling. He went on and on about his mother. He seems free while talking about her. His eyes seem to brighten up. "She used to read me books to fall asleep." he finally adds.

"She sounds lovely." I finally respond. I read to him until he fell asleep, and I moved to the floor with a pillow and blanket, but first double-checking to see if my door was locked.

Little O is running around the meadow playing. I look to the left of me, and I see a large oak tree with a woman sitting underneath holding a book in her hands. "Come on, Lorenzo!" she calls out to him. He goes to her obediently and sits. "I think you will like this book," she tells him and smiles. He rests his head on her shoulder as she reads

Alice's adventures in wonderland. "Once upon a time...." she reads as O flips the pages for her.

"Grandma, can I have a neckless like his?" asks Rose.

"yeah! me too!" Josie Beggs.

"Ask your parents," Grandma says. Both the girls look glumly at each other. *"now, if there are any more interruptions, I won't let you."* the grandma responds strictly. *"she reads as little O flips the pages...*

Chapter Twelve, Letters.

12

"Good Morning." O chimes.

"Good Morning." I chime back and yawn.

"Ready to go and get all the stuff he wants?" I nod. I leave the room to go and get ready for the day. When I come back, my door is open. Grant.

"Lia, why was your door closed?" Grant asks when I walk in.

"Um, it must have been the wind," where did he go? "I'm getting ready for the day, leave." he rolls his eyes and walks out. I lock the door and start to panic. Did he see O? I open the window and lookout. He's not there. Did he leave? I can feel my heart racing. I sit on my bed. Something grabs my ankle. I yelp. I hear him laugh. I curse at him. He laughs even harder. He struggles to get up. Now I laugh at him.

"Shut up," he says with a grin. We sit there quietly, listening for the front door to open and close. Once Gant leaves, we go downstairs to the kitchen and eat breakfast. I don't think I fully ate breakfast until a few days ago. Once we are done, we reread the list that Benjamin gave me.

"I think we can look in the attic for some stuff," I say. We head up to our old attic that is full of baby things and cobwebs. O picks up an old teddy bear.

"Do you remember me? It's Mr. Fuzzy pants. Have you come to rescue me from this old box?" he teases in a mocking tone. We both laugh. I pick up an old toy doll and toss it in an old empty cardboard box.

"What else can we get up here?" I ask, thinking out loud.

120

"Here's a box of kid's books," he says while standing in the back right corner. He reaches over other boxes and trips over something. I rush over and help him up.

"Are you alright?" I ask him.

"Yeah, I'm fine." He looks stunned at first, then confused. He moves the boxes that he knocked over to the other side of the room. "What's under here?" he asks. I look over and notice a latch on the floor.

"I'm not sure," I'm confused. "I don't think any of us ever noticed that," O opens the latch, there is a loud click. He swings the door open, and there is a medium-sized box inside. We pull the box over to an old table and a few chairs. He opens the box, and it is full of paper and a bunch of random objects. I grab the papers as he looks through the things. I sort the papers by the page numbers on the bottom right and start reading.

Journal entry .1. William Jones.

Today we sorted out plans for the future. Which I do not agree with any of them. The Lee family had made this place and is now setting ~~laws~~ rules. I think most of them are useless, a waste of time, and even cruel.

Journal entry .2.

They finished building the fence today. I wonder if they will make a gate. I would hate to be trapped here for the rest of my life. They started building houses and buildings too. They took all phones and devices away. I keep mine hidden in a box with most of my belongings.

Journal entry .3.

Now we are not allowed to leave, and if you have not gone into the fence, you would be executed. This is one of the many rules I hate.

Journal entry .4.

This will most likely be my last journal entry. I have not followed all the rules. These laws of Theirs are more like kids setting up rules for a board game. Here is a list of all the rules that they have set, and I have gotten to hear enough of the Lee family's secrets to start making a list.

1. You may not go ~~past~~ beyond the fence.
2. You may not have electronics.
3. you have to get your job picked between the ages of ~~14-18~~ 16-18
4. You can not speak of the old world or anything that lies beyond the fence.
5. You may not own more than 1 home.
6. You may not choose your job.
7. ~~You may not go visit the other side of the fence, or you get executed.~~

Lee family secrets.

There can be only one son in the Lee family at a time. The sons will become the governor. There shall be no daughters; if one is born, they will get executed.

There should be the job <u>Responsibility</u> in the bowl that holds all the jobs. Whoever receives the jobs will get threatened by the governor to have their family, friends, and themselves killed if they don't complete the following responsibilities.

Bring him a pocket knife, a picture frame, something gold, A rose, A bottle of paint, A children's book, A glass jar, A child's toy, A bracelet, A rope, A hairclip, and A watch. Once that is done, invite them to dinner and give them poisoning that will kill it and its family. For the wives and mothers of the sons, once the son is independent, she gets...

Responsibility

There are dried-up brown-red splotches on the paper blocking out the last few words. Blood. I feel burning tears running down my face.

"Lia, can you hear me?" he sounds concerned. I drop the papers, and they slowly fall to the ground. I can't move. I hear Grant.

"Lia, are you home?" he calls out to me. He's going to kill my family and me. O calls down to him frantically, and Grant comes rushing up the attic ladder. "Why are you here? And what did you do to her?" he exclaims at O. Why is their first reaction to someone upset is to freak out.

"I came here to help her find some things, and we found a door and a box and papers and some weird things," he is completely freaking out. "Then she read those papers and now this!" he concludes. Grant picks up the papers, and they read at the same time. O takes the papers. While turning red, he's practically shaking. Frantically he tries to get rid of the red stain. Tears fall from his face. "What happened to my mother!"

he yells as if the papers will him will give him answers. He searches the box for more. Grant stands there stunned.

Why is he doing this? He moves his feet and climbs back down the ladder. I get up and wipe my tears away. I should have known Benjamin would do such a thing. It should comfort O instead of him helping me for once. I walk over to him and hug him. He rests his head on my shoulder, and I hold him. After a few minutes, we gather all the stuff we found and make our way back to my room. I read for a bit and finally.

"I still have to get this stuff to Benjamin; if not, he will know we know something. We can make a plan. We can leave. We can run away." he looks up but does not speak. "I will get Grant to help now that he knows as much as us."

"What do you think he will do to everyone else if we leave? And how will we leave? Where will we go?" he found his voice and asks.

"I'm not sure. We will make a more detailed plan later." he nods. "We still have six days to figure everything out," I add. He closes his eyes and takes a deep breath.

"I should get back to my place for a while, so Benjamin does not wonder why I am gone a full day,"

"Okay, be safe," I walk him to the front door and say goodbye. I head to Grant's room and knock on the door.

"Can I come in?" I ask. He does not answer; I go in anyway. "You know why I had to lie? Just this time, I found out even more than I expected, I guess." His eyes were red, and he would not look into mine. "We are making a plan to get out of this place."

"Can't we fight back! Why do we have to run! I want to stay; this is my home!" he cries. I sit next to him

"Some things we can't fight," I tell him. "We have to figure out a plan before the 23rd," I leave and go into my room for the rest of the night.

Over the next few days, O comes every night in secret. We read and go over plans. After every night, he goes back to Benjamin's to check in and to make nothing seem unusual. I still have no bad dreams, but it was the same one every day now. The mom, the boy that looks like O, the book, the blue sapphire the mom wears, and the same meadow with the tree. We plan on leaving this place the morning of the dinner.

It's now the 20th. Grant comes into my room in the afternoon.

"Why is he here? When did he get here?" he asks, confused.

"He got here a while ago," I answer.

"Hello, brother of Lia," he greets politely even though they both don't agree with anything. Quite frankly, they don't like each other.

"We have less than three days to figure everything out. Where we are going, when, how, what we are going to do with Benjamin, what's going to happen to everyone else." I state listing out only a few of the things we need to worry about.

"What are you going to do about mom and dad?" Grant asks me.

"I'm not sure; let's split up the list so we can figure stuff out faster. O and I will find out what we are going to do about

Benjamin. I will figure out where we are going and how we will get there. Is there anyone important that we will bring into this?

Speak now, or don't mention it again." I reply.

"Suzen," O says right away. I still feel uneasy about her.

"Are you sure?" I ask him; he nods.

"Who's Suzen?" Grant asks. He is fidgeting his hands.

"She's a friend of mine, and she used to be the last one to get responsibilities," O answers.

"If she was the old one, why is she not dead? And there hasn't been another person with that job in twenty years, Benjamin would have been in the final schooling still." Grant responds.

"She must not have met his requirements," I answer for him. "I think Diane should come," I add.

"Why is that?" Grant asks.

"Do you really think only the four of us can survive together? We should get at least one more person."

"I have a friend," Grant says. "He has a farmer for his job, so he would know about plants." I nod.

"Can we trust him with these secrets?" I ask him. He shakes his head up and down.

"No matter what, at the latest, we have to leave Thursday morning; that's when Benjamin wants me to stay for 'dinner,'" I say while making quotation marks with my hands.

"We have to get everyone to meet us up at the tree pile tomorrow." O chimes in. "you and I will go and give Benjamin all the things he wants tomorrow also." he adds, directing to me.
"He won't make you stay for dinner if he already planned it for it to be Thursday, but he will do everything in his power to

make sure you are there. He is well planned and organized," he admits. I agree with him.

"What and where is the tree pile?" Grant asks.

"Follow the left side of the fence, then turn right when you see a big oak tree, then you will see like twenty fallen trees with very few standings. You will bring everyone there, but my friend Suzen of course." O replies.

"Over the next couple of days, I will gather supplies we need." I assert. "If there is anything personal you need, bring it in your bag. That includes clothes." That's all we talk about that night. Grant goes back into his room, and I sit on my bed with glazed eyes thinking. I walk over to my desk and pull out my copy of Shakespeare's Hamlet, a few pieces of paper, and a pen. O looks at me curiously, but I don't give him any explanation. I just started to write.

To mom and dad,

I love you, never forget that. Us leaving is the safest way for us all to live. Hide, leave, run, I don't care what you choose, just be safe. Protect yourself. Just know that we are okay, and you will be too. Don't let the governor find you; he is evil and horrible. He will try to kill you both, don't let him even come close enough to let that happen. Everything will be okay. Do not try to find us; we will be safe if we are not all ready. Shakespeare's hamlet states, "there is nothing either good or bad, but thinking makes it so." Nothing good will happen to us, but nothing terrible will happen to us; try to forget us, so you don't have to think of us hurt or anything worse, start a new life, try to be happy. I know you named me Ophelia not just because of hamlet but because it means help. You choose it because I looked so small and helpless when I was young. I'm not young and helpless anymore. I am strong and brave. We know you love us and know we love you.

Ophelia.

I finished signing off the letter and stuck it in the book. I hid the book in my bookshelf till I know when I have to leave it out to be found. I feel my face go red, and I blink back my tears.

They will be okay.

Chapter Thirteen, The Plan.

13

O is already gone; he left a note saying he went to his house early to pack. I should pack my things too. I pack all the appropriate clothing I can find—clothes for when it's cold and clothes when it's hot. I will also pack a few books, including the first book me and O read together. Then I throw my little bag of toiletries and my toothbrush inside. I grab a larger bag and start packing essentials that everyone will need. Many blankets, some small pillows, toiletries, paper and pens, water bottles, old rope from an old swing set, three boxes of matches, as many cans of food I could find, a new pocket knife, towels, flashlights, a few watches, and some wire. I went to the kitchen and ate breakfast. Grant sits next to me and drinks his coffee.

"Shoot!" I exclaim.

"What?" he asks, confused. I rush out of my seat. I grab the box of stuff for Benjamin and the box of stuff from the hidden door. I pack the stuff for Benjamin in a bag that I don't like and add the stuff from the hidden door into the other bags with all the essential things. By the time I'm done, I am exhausted. I lie on my back on my bed, staring at the ceiling. I will miss this place. Even the days and nights of fear. Why were those rules made anyway? Who was that man who wrote those journal entries? What's the point of killing us?

"Lia!" Grant calls for me. "The idiot is here," I roll my eyes.

"The only idiot here is you." I hear O throw back at him. I don't feel like stopping there bickering. I go downstairs to greet him and bring him back to my room. "Is this everything?" he asks me.

"Mostly." I sigh. He gives me a sad look.

"Get some rest," he tells me. I shake my head.

"I'm not tired." he can tell I'm lying, but he knows I won't until everything is done.

"Let's head to Benjamin's then," he says. I stop and almost walk straight past Grant.

"Bring everyone there in 2 hours," I advise.

"-kay," he replies out of focus.

"Did you hear me?"

"Yeah, yeah, bring everyone there in a few hours," he responds. O and I start our way to Benjamins. When we are almost there, he stops walking.

"Benjamin will think it's suspicious if we show up together again." I nodded and kept walking. He trails far behind me. When I get to the house's steps, I look behind me, and he's not there anymore. I walk to the sitting room and sit. I told one of the maids to get Benjamin. He walks into the room and looks surprised.

"You came early," he says with his eyebrows raised.

"Yes, I did," I assure him. He sits in the chair in front of me.

"You are still coming for dinner Thursday," he asks.

"Yes." I hand him the old bag with all the things he had asked for. He looks inside and gives me a nod.

"You can leave now." he asserts.

"Have a good day," I add. I walk out of the house, and I immediately felt calmer than I was inside. I meet O at the end of the path.

"We need to get Suzen." he decides. "Your brother would not know where to find her," he adds. I become hesitant. "Okay." is all I answer. We walk past the tree pile and head to the mostly empty buildings. When we stop at her building, O knocks on the door. I get an uneasy feeling. She opens the door, and she greets us.

"Suzen, will you come and take a walk with us?" O asks.

"Why?" she asks.

"We will explain when we get there," he replies. She looks annoyed.

"Fine." she agrees. We walk back to the tree pile, and everyone else is just arriving too.

"Ophelia? Why am I here?" Diane questions me. The boy my brother invited had the same question.

"Let's sit," I say, gesturing to one of the fallen trees that has not started to rot.

"Why…" Diane starts again.

"Shh." Grant interrupts her. She rolls her eyes. Grants almost like an older brother to her too.

"Can all of you promise me you won't go telling people about what I'm about to say?" I ask.

"Fine," Diane says.

"Yes." Everyone else replies calmly. I take in a jagged breath.

"We have to leave this place," I say as calmly as I can. Everyone starts to talk to each other.

"What!"

"Why!"

"No!" I look over to O for any assistants. Finally, he steps in.

"The governor is my father, and he will try to kill all of her friends and family," he says right away. Everyone went quiet.

"Why am I included in this? I don't even know any of you besides Grant!" the boy that my brothers brought yells.

"We are getting to that point," Grant says. I reach in my back pocket and get the papers from the man named William Jones. I hand the papers to the boy, who was standing in the middle. The three of them huddled together and read the paper. They look up all at the same time.

"What about your parents?" Diane asks me.

"I wrote them a note that I will give them before we leave," I respond.

"I assumed you could help us because you work on a farm," Grant says. "You would know a lot about plants," he adds.

"Would you consider going?" O asks Suzen. She nods.

144

"Diane?" I add. She also nods.

"Jack?" Grant calls on.

"I guess,"

"What's the plan?" Diane asks.

"On Thursday morning, we will meet here and then cut a hole through the fence. No one packs a lot, only essential things, but bring any canned food if you can. I have already packed blankets, as much food as I could find, and other things that are essential to all of us." I conclude. The three of them depart, and O decides to stop at his place. So, it is just Grant and me walking home.

"Why did this have to happen to us?" he asks to no one in particular. I sigh.

Chapter Fourteen, Anger.

Grant's view.

14

We walk the rest of the way home in silence. "Why did this have to happen to us?" I ask out loud to no one in particular. Lia sighs. We walk home in silence.

The moment I get home, I walk up the stairs and start packing my bag. I pack all the clothes I need, and I pack a smaller bag with my bathroom things. I pack my water bottle and also my blanket. Do I need anything else? Lia already packed all the canned food we have. I guess I'll go to the attic to look around and see if there is anything we missed. I pull the rope that opens the door, pulls down the ladder, and steps up to the top and onto the floor. I walk over to the latch where they found all of the things from the man once named William Jones. Then I leaned down on all fours and looked around in the hole. There is something taped to the side. What is that? Could it have been mentioned in the journal entries? Is it dangerous? I pick it up and

I'm extremely cautious. It is a thin rectangle with one button on the bottom and three buttons on the side.

"Lia! Come up here." I call her.

"What?" she asks me when she finally gets up the ladder.

"Do you know what this is?" I ask her. She tilts her

head. "No, where did you find it?" she replies.

"Under the door where you guys found the other objects," I answer.

"Hmm." She walks over and takes the thing from my hands. She turns it in her hands and examines it. "Maybe this is the thing called a phone like what in the letters said," she says. She paces around the room and looks at the thing. "Is there anything else in there?" she asks, pointing towards the door. I look inside again. Next to where the 'phone' is, there was a black cable with what looks like a medal at the ends. Now there is nothing left inside.

"Here," I say, handing her the cable.

"I'm putting this with the other things." she decides. She goes downstairs, and I keep poking around to see what I can grab, but all I can find are old blankets. I put my bags inside Lias' room. I walk down the stairs and head to the door to take a walk to clear my mind. I open the front door, and O is standing there with a fist in the air, about to knock on the door. Why does he make me so furious?

"Hello, idiot," I greet him. He rolls his eyes and walks in. "So, you're not even going to wait for me to invite you in?" calm yourself. I can feel my face going red. "So, you're not going to talk? Is the head of yours screwed on, right?" I add. He starts to get red too. Why am I still talking? He did not do anything yet, so why am I upset? "Oh, I'm sorry, did I offend you?" I ask in a mocking tone.

"Shut up," he advises clenching his teeth.

"Why, what are you going to do?" I ask him. Bang. He hits me. Not just hits me, he punches me, and I fall. He does not stop; he keeps going. I hear someone walk down the stairs.

"O!" Lia screams. He does not listen. "Stop!" I can hear the fear in her voice. "Lorenzo!" she yells. He stops. He looks up at her. Tears start to form in his eyes. He opens his mouth to speak, but it seems that he can't find his voice. He gets up from the floor and runs out of the house. "Are you okay?" she asks me. I nod. "What did you say to him?" she adds.

"What did I say to him? What did I say!" I repeat myself. "You're asking me when he was the one who attacked me!"

"Grant!" she interrupts me. "Did you forget that you hurt him before? Kicked him! Punched him! He almost broke his nose! And what did he do? He did not fight back; he never would hurt someone without reason. So, what did you do!" I am speechless; she never yells at me. Is she telling the truth? Why was I so mad at nothing?

My head is screaming. She storms out of the house; I watch her run down the paths after O from the window. How did she find out about the day at the beach? Did he tell her? Was it obvious that it was me? I groan in frustration. Why? I went back to my room and sat at my desk. I stay staring at the blank gray walls. When I finally start to relax, I get up and go to the bathroom to look in the mirror.

I have a black eye and a fat lip. How am I supposed to hide this from my mother? I shake my head. I decide to take a walk. I walk around the park and try not to think of him. It does not work. What's wrong with me? Why do I get so angry? I walk around asking myself these questions over and over again in my head for about an hour. Once I finally got back, no one was home yet. Thank god. I head to the bathroom and open my mother's makeup bag. I have never touched makeup before. I try my best to rub in all the different powders and pastes in the bag to try to make myself look almost back to normal. My black eye is now only a light blue shadow. Finally, at least it only looks like I'm exhausted. Better than a black eye. I sigh and walk back to my room. What's wrong with me? I lay on my bed and stare at the ceiling. Eventually, I fall asleep.

Chapter Fifteen, Hurt.

O's view.

15

I part from the group and decide to go back to Benjamin's house and see if I can find anything else to pack. I don't want to be there; I need to be with Lia. I hope I can get inside before Benjamin sees me. I get to the steps and open one of the large doors. Nope. There he is at the other side of the door.

"Hello, son." he greets me. I take in a shaky breath.

"Hello," I respond.

"Where have you been?" he asks me.

Responsibility

"I have been at the beach," I answer right away.

"You better not be getting into any trouble, boy," he says strictly; I nod. "Let's take a walk," he commands. I follow obediently. I know exactly what's going to happen. It's going to be like almost every time he says that. I try to slow my shaky breathing. We walk around for half an hour before we stop at the old abandoned building we go to every time. We step inside, and it is dark.

The moment the door closes, he punches me on my side, then the other. He continues punching me and kicking me until I finally fall. I feel like a child. I cry. He finally stops and just stares at my pathetic self. He looks at me with disappointment. Why me? Why now? I need to stand, but I can't. I just lay there and weep.

"Crying like a baby," he says with disappointment. "I thought I taught you well." he shakes his head. "I take that back; I did teach you well; you are just dumb." he laughs at his own stupid comment. "Finish the rest of the hour for me. I think I'm done," he adds. Two men walked over to me and did the same as Benjamin did. I broke.

"Mom!" I scream like a little boy. Benjamin turns around the doorway; he was about to leave.

"What did you say, boy!" he laughs darkly. "Your mother is dead!" He looks me in the eyes. "You made her so tired she decided to catch a sickness and die just to get away from you!" he yells at me.

"No!" I yell back. "She died from a sickness you gave her!" I scream.

"No, what makes you think that?" he asks, quieter this time.

"You're evil!" I give up after that. He walks away and lets the men continue to hurt me. Why does he do this? I never yelled for my mother like that. Not once. I stay silent the rest of the time. Benjamin and the men always made sure to never hurt me from my neck up. He is always scared that someone would find out he hurts me. He's a coward.

Finally, the hour is up. The moment they let me go, I run to the beach even though my legs hurt. I take a deep breath, and a sharp pain runs through my lungs. I try to practice a fake smile, at least for when I see Lia. I don't want her to worry about me or anyone but herself. It won't be hard for me not to smile when I see her. She is the only one who can make me smile. She makes me laugh and feel happy for once. I need her for that. I'm finally calm enough to walk to her house. I put a fist in the air to knock on the door, but the door opens first.

"Hello, Idiot." Grant greets me. I ignore him and walk into the house. "So, you're not even going to wait for me to invite you in?" he asks me. Is he trying to piss me off? "You're not even going to talk? Is the head of yours screwed on, right?" he asks. "Oh, I'm sorry, did I offend you?" he adds in a mocking tone. I felt my face go red. I need to make sure I stay calm for Lia; I keep repeating in my head. It's not working.

"Shut up," I tell him, and I clench my teeth.

"Why, what are you going to do?" he asks me. I snap. I punch him and kick him. It hurts doing so, I am sore from Benjamin, but I don't stop. I hear someone, but I don't listen. I finally hear her now.

"Lorenzo!" she screams. I stop and look at her. I feel tears starting to form in my eyes. I ran out the door and onto the path. She hates me, I'm sure of it. Why did I do that? Why did he have to open his stupid mouth? I keep running, and I don't stop. I run to the opposite side of the fence and collapse. I want to scream, but I restrain myself.

"Why?" is all I can say to myself. Why does Benjamin hurt me? Why does he insult my mother? Why did he kill her? I almost scream again, but I stop myself. I look up from the ground, and I see Lia running after me. I put my head down in embarrassment.

Responsibility

"What happened?" she questions me. I don't answer. "Are you okay?" I look up; she looks scared. Is she scared of me? "I'm sorry for whatever Grant said," she adds.

"I'm sorry." is all I can choke out. She looks confused.

"It's not your fault." She tells me. I scoff, and I get up from the ground. I start to walk away, so Lia grabs my sleeve. "I said it's not your fault," she repeats.

"What do you mean it's not my fault!" I yell, then continue. "I hurt him, and all you can say is that "it's not my fault!" well, It is my fault, I punched him! I kicked him!" I say and try to walk away again.

"Stop!" she yells back. I don't like it when she yells. She hates me. "Fine, it is your fault, but that means it's Grant's fault; it could even mean it was my fault!" she looks frightened.

"It's not-" I try to say, but she interrupts me.

"Don't you say it back to me now," she says, a little bit calmer. "It's none of our faults, okay?" I was looking into her eyes now. I still feel that it's my fault, but I drop it.

"Okay." I finally agree. She nods. We walk to the fallen trees, and we sit staring at the sky. "How should we get out of the fence?" I ask her.

"We will somehow cut a hole on the bottom with a saw or whatever tool I find," she says. She must have put a lot of thought into this. She's shivering.

"Are you cold?" I ask her, knowing she'll say no.

"No, I'm fine." She lies to me. I roll my eyes and stand up to take my sweater off. My shirt had lifted when I took the sweater off. She gasps.

"I thought Grant didn't hurt you this time?" she says like a question. She came closer to me and lifted my shirt just enough to see my right side. I push her hand away gently and pull my shirt down. "Why are you covered in bruises?" she questions me.

"It's nothing," I say. She looks me in the eyes with disbelief.

"Don't lie to me," she demands me. I'm not lying, at least. Usually, it's worse.

"It's not from Grant, and I'm fine." I try to reassure her.

"It was Benjamin, Wasn't it?" I look at the ground. I don't answer because she knows the answer. I hand her the sweater.

We don't sit back down; we just stare at each other for a minute. We continue in silence, and we walk back to her house, get to the door, and walk-in. Grant is at the door immediately.

"I'm sorry," he says right away. I nod.

"I'm sorry," I apologize back. We say no more, and Lia and I walk up the stairs into her room.

Chapter Sixteen,

Memories. Lia's view.

16

I should have been downstairs when the fight happened. I sit at my desk, and O sits on my bed. I want Benjamin to go away and for us to stay. He hurts O; he shouldn't deserve to be here. I groan in frustration. He picks up one of the books on my nightstand and starts to read out loud. I turn around towards my desk and listen to him. I picked up a piece of paper and began to draw the beautiful meadow from my dreams. I like to draw, of course not as much as reading, but I still draw every few days.

He pauses reading and walks over to me.

"What's this?" he asks me.

"Nothing," I reply. He grins.

"I didn't know you can draw," he says and looks as if he is impressed. I roll my eyes.

"I can't; they are just pictures," I say; I'm not exactly a fan of people knowing what I am good at. They will think too much and expect too much from me. He grabs the other pieces of paper that were crammed in some of the drawers on the desk.

They were all old drawings. "Give them back," I advise. I reach for them, and he holds them up in the air where I can't reach them.

I'm getting annoyed. "I said give them back." He laughs. I can't help but grin.

I continue to try to reach for the papers, then Grant walks into the room. He gives us a weird look and walks out. We burst into laughter. He gives up and hands me the papers. We sit back down and calm ourselves. He starts reading again, and I continue to draw the meadow. I finally put the paper down and I sit on the bed next to him. It's 10 pm; he finishes the end of one of the chapters in the book. I lay down and fall asleep.

It's the same dream that I have every night. Wait. Why won't he climb the fence? "Hurry!" I scream. He stands there afraid. "Climb!" he stands there unmoving. "Come on!" nothing. "Please!" they get him, the two men in suits. "No!" I screamed as loud as I could.

I wake up in my bed crying. O is not there. Where is he? I start hyperventilating. My head is screaming. Where is he? He finally walks back into the room.

"What's wrong? Why are you crying? Are you okay?" he questions me in a panicked voice.

"I'm fine, just a bad dream," I answer. I finally calm down. "Please don't leave me alone again?" I ask him.

"Never," he replies and gives me a sad smile. I fell back to a dreamless sleep.

I wake, but I don't move. I stare at the ceiling, thinking. This is my last full day in this place. It's a hell hole now, but I am still going to miss it here. I am not dying, but my life is flashing before my eyes. *When I lost my first tooth. My mother and father would read me to sleep. The dull days at school. All the time, Diane and I snuck out to play at the beach. The times when Grant and I chased each other around the house playing tag - you're - it, and admittedly getting scolded by our mother. The nights at the dinner table. The funny and sometimes scary stories my father told me. The fantasy world I went to when my mother and I read Shakespeare. When Grant and I raced to school together. The times when I argued with Grant about the dumbest things.*

I bite my lip and try to hold back the tears that I know are trying to escape from my eyes. I feel the knot in my throat starting to form. O fell asleep with his arm around me, so I carefully moved his arm to go to the bathroom to wash my face.

Responsibility

I am halfway across the room, and he asks me, "where are you going?" I breathe as quietly as I can.

"Just to the bathroom, I'll be right back." I cringe at how badly my voice breaks. Without waiting for him to respond, I quickly walk to the bathroom. I turn on the faucet to drown out any sounds. I sit on the floor and quietly sob. I never want to leave. I calm myself; I stand up, walk over to the sink, wash my face. I turn off the facet, not trying to waste any more water.

I walk back into my room, and O doesn't say anything. He walks over to me and hugs me.

"I know this is hard for you. It will be okay, and everyone will be just fine." he tries to reassure me. I take in his familiar scent that makes me feel safe. A scent that is just his. There is nothing that can describe it. It's him. He lets go of me, and I slowly walk to the kitchen. I look at every familiar grain wood floor. Every detail on the wallpaper. Every painting on the walls.

We sit at the table in silence, and we eat. Will we even survive out there? Grant walks into the kitchen with the same glum expression on his face. He sits between O and me, I'm guessing purposely to keep us apart.

"Why does he have to sleep here?" he questions me. I close my eyes and try to ignore him.

"I think we should check in with everyone today, make sure they are or aren't backing out. We have to make sure they are ready and safe." O says. I nod in agreement.

"I'll check on Diane, Grant checks on Jack, and O checks on Suzen." I leave the table right away, put on my shoes, and went out the door heading towards Diane's house. I can't stand to be in that house for another minute. I walk up to the steps of her house and knock on the door. "Diane?" I pause. "Are you home?" She opens the door.

"Hey." She greets me.

"Are you still in for tomorrow?" I ask her. She nods.

Responsibility

"Are you packed?"

"Yes." she looks upset.

"Are you okay?" I ask, trying to ease the tension.

"Yeah, you?" she sighs. I give her a quick smile, not knowing what to say.

"Don't worry about me, do you remember the plan?" nod. "Will you be able to meet me at the spot two hours earlier than what we said?" nod. "Please don't tell anyone either," I ask in a pleading voice. Nod. "Bye." I finally say.

"Bye," she replies.

I walk back to my place, and no one is home. I sit on my bed and contemplate what we are going to do when we escape from this hell. I walk over to my dresser and pick up my old toy. It has two half circles for ears and one large circle in the middle of the face with string sewed in the mouth and nose. There are two button eyes, and it has two arms and two legs.

N.S.F

My mother has always called it a teddy bear. I hug it for a moment and think about the times when I was young, in my bed clutching the bear in fright after bad dreams.

"Lia?" I hear O call from the door.

I walk out of my room and meet him halfway down the stairs. "You left the door opened," he tells me with a confused voice.

"Oh, must have forgotten," I say. We walk into my room, and he sits on my bed. I move to my desk, and he starts to read like usual. I take out a piece of paper and start writing.

Dear Lorenzo,

If you are reading this, that means something happened to me. If that something is death, then I have to ask this of you. Don't grieve over me; just keep moving and make sure you are safe. Make sure my brother does not lose his mind, well at least make sure he is eating and taking care of himself. Please. I love you. -Lia

N.S.F

I fold the piece of paper and hide it in my book that also hides the note for parents. "What did Suzen say?" I ask, interrupting him. He folds down the corner of the page he is on for bookmark, and he closes the book.

"She is coming, and she's ready to go; what about your friend?" he replies.

"Same with Diane." he nods. Why is he not upset about leaving? Grant walks through the front door. It's 5 pm. "What took you so long?" I ask him.

"Did You know Jack's house is all the way in front of the east fence?" he informs us. We live oppositely; we live near the west fence. "He is still in for the plan," Grant adds. Me and O walk back into my room. We sit on my bed, and I began to read to him this time. I hear my mom get home. After a while, she calls Grant and me for dinner.

"I'll be right back," I tell him. I walk down to the dining room and greet my mom. "May I eat in my bedroom today?" My mom looks at me funny.

"I guess. Is there something wrong?" she asks me.

"No, I'm just tired and would like to lay down."

"Okay, get some rest." my mom replies. I walk back to my room and shut the door right away.

"Here, I'm not hungry," I tell O and hand him the plate of veggies and chicken.

"Are you sure?" he asks me. I give him a smile and nod. I do not feel like eating. I feel sick. I sit back at my desk and watch him eat. "This is amazing; tell your mom it's delicious." he says but then immediately adds, "well, I guess don't," he says, laughing nervously. I grin and shake my head. I turn around to face the desk, and I start to read again. I hear a knock on the door.

O immediately sits up to climb out my window if it's one of my parents.

"It's me. Can I come in?" Grant asks from behind the door. O immediately relaxes his shoulders but does not lay back down.

"Yeah." my voice invites. He walks in and shuts the door.

"What will we tell mom and dad?" he asks. I sigh.

"I wrote them a note," I answer. He nods and heads out the door. "Wait, Grant," I say and walk out into the hallway. "Get some sleep, okay?" I tell him.

"Okay, you too," he replies. I hug him and walk back into my room. It's only 9 pm, but I should listen to what Grant told me. I lay on my bed on the opposite side of O, and I try to fall asleep.

It's the dream. The boy and I are playing in the meadow again, and I sit by the big oak tree, listening to the almost music-like laughter coming from our happiness. Everything changed in the blink of an eye. It's dark. Almost all the trees have fallen except the big oak tree. It's the tree pile in this place; that's why it looks so familiar. I start to cry.

N.S.F

Why did this place have to ruin my only good dream? I sit up and stare at the wall trying to fall back to sleep, and hopefully a dreamless one.

"Are you okay?" I hear O whisper. I turn around and bury my face into the pillow, ignoring him. "I love you, Lia," he whispers. My heart feels full. I do not say anything, guessing that he thinks that I am asleep. I finally fall back into a dreamless sleep.

Chapter Seventeen, Won but lost.

17

I Stand up from my bed, hoping I don't wake him.

Move to my desk and take out a piece of paper and a pen. *Dear O,*

> *I'll be back soon; I have to finalize a few plans.*
-*Lia.*

I set the note next to him on the bed and grab my bag. I take the book where I hid the notes and stuff it in my bag. Grant is sitting at the table in the kitchen.

"Where are you going?" he asks me with a worried tone in his voice.

Responsibility

"To finalize all the plans, I'll be back soon," I state and make my way to the door.

"Be safe," he cautions me. I give him a short smile, and I walk out of the house to the shed. I pick up some old plant trimmers and throw them in my bag. I make my way to the fallen trees to meet Diane there. I walk fast and quietly, so no one hears me or sees me. I get there, and she's already here.

"What took you so long?" she asks with wide eyes.

"Sorry, I woke up late." She relaxes a bit. "you know you don't have to come with us, right?"

"I know; what did you need?" she asks.

"Here." I tell her, and I hand her the note for O. "please give this to O if anything happens to me."

"Who is O?" she asks.

"The boy with black hair," I answer. She nods and takes it from my hand. "Here," I say. We walk over to the fence, and I take the plant trimmers out. I assume that they are sharp enough to cut through the silver wire of the fence. I cut just enough so it can open it like a door, but it can close and look normal. "Thank you."

"No problem." she says."

"I want to get everyone else at my house early today. Do you want to come?" she nods, and we head towards the place where Suzen lives. After what seems like forever, we get to her building.

I knock on the door. "Who is it!" I hear Suzen yell.

"It's me, O's friend Lia," I say back. She opens the door. "Are you ready to go? I want to get everyone to my house before we have to leave." I add.

"Yeah," she answers. She closes the door to unlock the chain lock, and she steps outside with a backpack. We walk unseen to my house. We step through the door, and it seems that O and Grant have a stare-off.

"Hello, Suzen, Diane." O stands up and greets them.

"Grant, can you go and bring Jack here?" I ask him. Then Jack walks through the door. "Never mind then," I add.

"We should leave in an hour," O says.

"Do you want to help me get the bags upstairs?" I ask O. he gives a smile then nods. We get to my bedroom, and I find my voice to finally say this. "I love you too." he smiles and looks down. His face goes red. I walk over to our bags and pick two up; O gets the last two. We go back downstairs and put the bags on the dinner table. I open the bag that holds the items that were in the attic with the journal.

"This is some of the items that were mentioned on these papers we showed you a few days ago." They all look and examine the objects.

"What if they are dangerous?" Jack asks.

"Nothing has happened since we found them, and they have been in the attic for a long time beforehand, so I don't think so," Grant says.

We sat in silence for the next 40 mins.

"We should get going," O advises. We all go outside and stand there for a few seconds.

"Wait, I'll be right back," I say. I go back into the house and open the book with the note for my parents. I lay the book and note it neatly on the table for them to find. I take in one last familiar breath of my home. I walk back outside, and we head to the tree pile. We are almost there.

"Wait!" I hear my father yell. All of our heads turned.

"Dad?" my brother yells.

"What are you doing here?" I ask. "It's not safe; leave, go home,"

"Why? What's going on? Why are you leaving!" he asks. "Nothing, we will be fine, go home." my brother says. We all continue walking as Grant, and I are trying to get our father to go home.

"Who's that?" O asks quietly. "Is someone following us, or is that a friend of yours?" he adds.

"What?" My dad gives us a confused look. We turn around, and there is a man in a suit behind us.

"Run!" O yells; we all run to the fence. My dad is way slower than us from his old age, but he is still ahead of the man. I turn around again, and the man is holding up what looks like a metal pipe with a handle attached to it.

Boom. my ears are ringing, and there is smoke. The some finally start to dissipate, and I see my father lying in front of me in a puddle of dark red liquid. I scream. I try to run to him, but I can't. Someone is holding me back. I don't stop screaming. The man is still heading towards us. I want to hurt him for what he has done. O picks me up, and I struggle to get down, but I can't.

I feel numb. We get through the fence where I cut with the plant cutters. We are free.

"Grandma!" yells rose.

"Then what happened!" yells Josie.

"Be patient." the grandma says. "The story will get better," she adds calmly. The girls were sitting up straight with anticipation.

"Is this a real story?" Rose asks.

"You ask again once I'm done reading," Grandma responded. "They were beyond the fence free…"

Ophelia Waters, 16 years old. Nick-name, Lia. Friends are Grant, Lorenzo, and Diane.

Grant Waters, 18 years old. No nickname. His friends are Lia, Diane, and Jack.

Lorenzo Lee, 17 years old. Nickname is O. his friends are, Suzen and Lia.

N.S.F

Diane Henderson, 16 years old. No nicknames. Her friends are Lia and Grant.

Other characters include:

Suzen Johnson.

Diane Henderson.

Jack Young.

Amy Waters.

Elizabeth Lee.

Kevin Waters.

Benjamin Lee.

Nancy Hamilton.

Book 2 out of the Responsibility series.

N.S.F

I walk quickly in between Grant and O. Hot tears fall from my face silently. I don't make any noise; I feel numb. It was my fault. I was the one who left the note. I should have made sure what time he would come home. It should have been

me in place of him. Let me back up a tad.

Long story short, once a year, there is a ceremony, kids 16-18 get to have someone pick a job written on a piece of paper from a large glass jar, and yes, it is entirely random. I got the job called 'responsibility.' the governor ordered me around, making me bring random things to him. Things he didn't need, all to attempt to kill me. Why might you ask? Well, I don't know. When I figured out how to save my family and friends, I lost my father. What was that thing the man had? It seemed like O knew what it was. How is Grant taking all of this? We start to slow our pace after an hour of going between running and walking. We are in the middle of what seems like thousands of trees.